BESTIAL MOUTHS

Brenda S. Tolian

Bestial Mouths © 2024 by Brenda S. Tolian

Published by Raw Dog Screaming Press
Bowie, MD

First Edition

Cover art copyright 2024 by Chlo'e Camonayan
chloecamonayan.com
Book Layout by Jennifer Barnes

Printed in the United States of America

ISBN: 978-1-947879-80-5
Library of Congress Control Number:
2024945612

RawDogScreaming.com

BESTIAL

MOUTHS

CONTENTS

Melioë 9

Asudem 11

Skinwalker Moon 14

Kombuto 16

Speak Nonsense 17

Eros Root 18

Acrobat Girl 21

Ouroboros 22

Chrome 23

Johnathan Fry 25

Inanna 27

Dead Gods 29

Jane 30

Open 32

Melancholy 33

Strzyga 35

Apple 38

Lilith 41

A Work in Progress 44

Impulse 46

Home 48

Copper 49

B-Girls 50

Crow Man.. 52

I Know... 54

Stone.. 55

A Dream 57

You.. 59

Coil... 60

Child.. 62

Haunted.. 64

Epar 66

Full Moon 68

Babylon.. 70

La Leth Laughs 72

Ytsirhc.. 73

Argona 75

Bones of word, Bone of Feather 77

Ninava 79

Poison Woman... 80

Opio-Cordyceps 82

December Mother.. 86

Tiamat Dreaming.. 89

Awake Now.. 94

DEDICATION

Dedicated to women and girls who are lost or missing, those who cling to independence and agency in a world that would take them away, those who wish to command their own bodies and minds, and those who have been silenced or told to be quiet.

She felt herself pulled into the nightmare—an effigy of an unhindered, unchained brain burning. The visions they followed. Give into the fear. It is only a dream, after all.

MELIOË

close your eyes love, let me swallow you down
into the darkness, into the ground
within the nightmare wrapped in the pain
everything is nonsense, nothing the same

cut me open
ripped—wide
my heart it is beating
whispered questions
why
this is where it started
the yawning divide
and this is how it ends
no one here
to cry

stories on paper
eventual end
baptism of blood
brought on by
sin
lies on the lips

cutting of nails
scrying the future
in mountain cut trails
hear the wind
moaning
the earth catches the heel
the bestial mouths
chanting dark spells
my body is changing,
into something else
this touch of madness
hot in the blood
words they are magic
in coming undone
beyond the veil
of dreaming and sleep
unraveling the secrets
i no longer keep

Asudem

tangle your hand
in the biting mouth,
her hair dances alive
slip it down slow
like rope
around the neck
don't be afraid
swing above
as you swung below
mastication of teeth
snapping of jaw
body and bone slip in the dark
eyes close
swimming the dark water

words muted
mid-song
virgins in love
virgins done wrong
naive they drink the wine
secrets spun anew
hard in the belly

like slippery stone
some things you tell
others you swallow
a story was told here
that was a lie

she begged in razor blades
knees bent like bird's wings
a delicate snap
broke at the neck
broke at the breast
feathers falling
like snow

there are things a girl never asked for
there are gazes given, ignored
some things are forcefully taken
cracked vessel left empty
a ghost on the acropolis floor

first penetration violent opening
next framing a whore veneration
like sugar on the tongues of the women in town
they created the stoning
in tandem with men
wives of the monsters
crawling on knees to the stone

where the innocent are tied
small sacrifices, tiny teeth
silence the story
behead the woman
sew serpents in stitches
right into the scalp
loop knots into the lips
silence is expected
let men wither under her shame
a moving veil
she will stone them all

Skinwalker Moon

Featured Poem/Poet-HWA Showcase vol. 8 2022

wolfskin, dry crackle, ragged fur
i taste you on the western wind
tension, four-limbed, two feet, two hands
below the peaceful pinyon, the sun has gone to blood
dripping down the Sangre de Cristo—i need you

gravel in my belly, hunger, mastication
claws grip the edge of the caldera
salt-sweat, and fear rolling over my tongue
howling to answering coyotes
the hunt, leaping over prickly pear
running until my chest bursts
i want you—in my throat

blade on belly, ragged teeth, count of twenty
slip skin, wet fabric, knitted cells
pulling the edges of your smiling meat mask
slow, warm, wet
neck, chin, and lip—i become you

drums, flickering pulse between sweat lined thighs

broken breastbone, cracking ribs, pull them wide

blood of sacred eagle

wings erect, you breathe through them

shake out of your skin, unzip your vertebrae

shiver, fine hair still erect

obsidian blade, peel away—what i need

slip into your body to become

breast of moon exhales over the dunes

warm and heavy your wet skin

claws sharpened on twisted cottonwood

my tongue licks your blood-flecked lips

elk white skull bone on my head

there is magic in the night

your muscle in my mouth

your warm heart in my hands

i am you

the you—that i never had

KOMBUTO

i find you unwind

like yarn

soft sinew

the color of red

tied to you

do not wander far

blood swallowed

forest floor

slants of light

blades of grass

salty blood

binds me

tight weaving

fleshy loom

tie me up

knotted into you

framework of tree

sewn into the limb

static in the air

body over you

reach but do not touch

impossible knot

Speak Nonsense

what is it
the
declining
      gentle
         slant
           of light
              return to
                  velvet soil
            dip the tongue
        draw up the cells
they glow brightly
 first red then brown
          when dried
            arise each night
           cutting teeth
         pushing out
      wet soil
    lichen soft
under fingertip
      like her skin
       that parts under claw
         I needed her

Eros Root

she awoke

tangled tight

in eros root

buried there

under the moon

above in the day

she could feel them

feel their little feet

gentle voices

children play

three little lambs

soft flesh tiny hands

pressing into the hollows between

filling the roots

with soft grass

doll's bed

her fingers probing

the soil above her tomb

each stone brittle bone

below her twisted cairn

she sings siren songs

lulling them to sleep

within the curve of the root

they pierce the skin

and drink them down

they look to be sleeping

but they are dead

stories told of in-between

witch below thrice tied

she calls to the babes

from her grave

a hunger to replace

the one that was stolen

blood in her mouth

at night she will reach

the child cradled in eros root

pulling the babe into her womb

curling her body around

waiting for the mother to scream

for the child that would never be found

but this was her way

as she was taught

memory of her burial there

payment of sorrow

she haunts the wood

it is the lady
of the eros root

creatures of furry limb
tickling the raw lip
insects crawling parting flesh
she was not herself
judas hung by the neck

eros root grew into her body
her arms, her breasts, her legs
she holds you now
don't move, little child
forever is nothing
for sins you must pay

Acrobat Girl

disjointed, contorted

i am the acrobat girl

scabbed fist

it fits, you know

right between cracked ribs

upside down

backward

sawing joints with broken mirrors

sixpence to make me dance

affix the galvanized wire

watch me move

i have no choice

i can't see you

my eyes and knees

cut out

to remain rubber

compliant

OUROBOROS

last night i was a beast
teeth and claws
the human quiet
chained up
ouroboros with no end,
arms, legs, mouth
connected
appetite ravenous
Luna applauded

gravitational pull
limbs like insects
teeth breaking
on bone and lip
inhale the smell
of darkened forest
ouroboros, they say
ouroboros, they tell us

CHROME

zombie apocalypse, or some such nonsense
emblazoned in black and white
frayed at the edges where the glue had obliterated,
on the shiny bumper of the old paint-chipped 84 LTD
i lean against it,
cause it's the only thing to lean against
in the chipped, broken pavement of ole Sally's liquor store
under the harsh glare of the one light that still worked
fluorescent with a faint electrical buzz
it leaves you feeling kind of empty, but you're not sure why
the windows are kinda hazy, built-up cigarette smoke and tar...
it was almost a dare to look inside
the bumper sticker was a truth to consider
tapping my foot, waiting, waiting, waiting
quick glance, nobody around,
not a soul—
old peeling vinyl with white threads like spider webs
the cloth of the ceiling held up with pennies
some shiny, some blackened.
receipts crumpled with remains of fast-food joints
cigarette butts,
strange smells of smoke, cloves, oil

if broken dreams had a smell
i hear the jingle of the bells on ole Sally's door
quickly back away—
the figure of a man, beginning his slow shuffle,
paper bag in hand,
hair wild in the night,
clothes rumpled,
too big for his awkward frame of old tired bones,
dry brittle and monochrome
It was his eyes, however, that caught me,
they seemed paint chipped and dull
like no one was really there
nobody home
a knock in the trunk, popped two inches wide
watery blink of emaciated eye
this is where the girls go when they disappear
on the road in the night
with no one to hear

Johnathan Fry

he liked to take pictures
women under streetlights
he staged them
with latex-gloved hands
to look doll-like alive
needle and golden thread
pulling the skin
into smiling
he tried but failed
to love them alive
he loved them on photo paper
he loved them in deep wells
he loved that the dead didn't cry
don't ever tell

the first time he did it
felt like a dream
caught his first flesh
walking sugar and cream
love at first sight
but he didn't ask
sweetness seemed to smile

when he brought down the axe
the places he opened
filled in with wax
ochre and paint
satin and shine
each chosen lovely
his for a time

tapeworm hunger
his terrible teeth
keepsakes of film
photographic sheets
there was an art to it
cultivated still
bound book, bound lady
muse to feed
and fulfill

INANNA

three souls know

impossibility

true union

does not exist

when power is taken

sister desert without her shoes

the pretender opens the door

the next :::: and the next

going lower

into the dark

naked

while Demuzi sits in ostrich blind posture

above in the summer

one setting less, the fragile mind burns black

no escaping the hook

step up, lower the neck

the point pierced

sewn-through

raised above the dais

sister death

demanded your ring

stole your shoe

you called in the demons
gave them
brisk command
replace him
in your place
hang him by the neck

DEAD GODS

i don't believe in gods anymore
the thin musculature of imagined limbs
the plump belly dancing
the gramophone flaring horn
seraphim with bloody maw
called us to rapture
we float, and they clutch
with piercing claws
redemption
dirty secrets sung
in gibberish
message repeats
incised once
particularly created
one for another
your whispered penance
relayed through anti-matter
practiced hope
in dead things

JANE

she seemed almost real
except for the wires coming out
flowing down
red, green, white
ending in a box on the floor
plugs in sockets
extended to walls
voice not robotic
synthesized perfect wit
her eyes lied
gave her away
the strange iridescent glow
certain deadness
she lacked a soul.
some men noticed
bristled with guilt
eyes of their wives
rushing to mind
in comparison
other men strangely comforted
no soul equal in absent attachment
neat and tidy plastic and silicone

easily cleaned
the expensive night wiped and reset
she was a machine
no different from any other loveless night
objectified for her parts only

Open

prone supplication

razor edge

like a zipper

undone

my spine

rolled

ripped out

stepping over

fabric of flesh

ah finally

finally

i can breathe

my lungs

they are like delicate paper wings

stretched out beside me

Melancholy

infinite sadness,

drowning

i died tonight

under those stars

under that moon

no one saw

my passing

the rewinding

slipping film out of flesh

moist soil in my mouth

my atoms separating

bursting into a million stars

no one saw

but you

what's your name?

your hands so intimate

around my neck

grunting

until my bones crack

was i special?

was it my hair?

floating in pond water

you watch from the sand
my last living visions
are you licking your hand?

STRZYGA

black holes follow

        conjure swallow

            the

                bitter mint

     scratching   twisting

         skin   head

         her body a scythe

   crouching

        on

        the ceiling (her head twists around, there is no soul in her eye)

            maw sawing

through
fleshy
bits

Incoherent   mantras

       crawling

         on

          bloody

            knees across glass

trying
 to
grow
small

someone let her in

pushed a hand through:::::::::::::::::::::::::::::::

the salt

slicing

wrist

blood

in

her

mouth

licking

the

sacred

salt

line

harems   are   never   peaceful

places of   grape   and feather

blackened

eyes bit lip

two

hearts are eaten   (they did not listen)

she craves

more

hunger   boils hellfire and acid

in her belly

in

the (you are doomed if you think to possess her)

cage

of

her

chest I hear their last breath

whispering

the strzyga's

secret name:::::::::::(hush)

but never

speak it

she will know

hear you

find you

wear you

Apple

you spout incantations like delicate threaded leaves

fibers of creation looping through the teeth

twirling around the neck

vertebrae centipede north and south

never to be the same again

dividing   pulled apart

roses in the garden where it V's

spiders perch with rough hairs,

venom on the articulated fangs—or so your mother said,

is pierced and torn asunder

melting into throaty caramel warmth.

you have never felt this before.

the muscle undulates

you wish you still had eye teeth—you are starving.

ribbon, blood, swirls, and ties

behind eyelids

beneath the skin

gravitational cyclone

spinning strong

eating the sun until it's broken

are you broken?

events swimming on horizon

feeling is eternal, delicate

eventually broken—you cannot hold on

They took your eyeteeth

trailing blood on the thigh

bleeding for seven days

pleasure, pain, pantomime

fingers dip into the soft

undefended tight slit

mouth-like

hungry

tongue over every curve and ridge

lawful mate

container of cracked

glass and plate

sky ripped apart

broken covenant

salt and sweat

lubrication of lock and key

Eve crept along the sunset shadow

nibbling on toes,

easing between thighs

you felt her slip between the both of you

a fractal, a pattern

observation

combination

golden ratio curling around cock and breast

her head revolving hungry

her finger deep in your throat
husband presses into her side
until he is molting with her
sheding the skin
fingers gripping ass and neck until your hips move without thought
Eve turns ratcheting until he is on her
within her, tail wound around his chest
you spill out like seed on the floor gnawing bone
you watch as they fuck
two animals fighting for dominance
power in appearing weak
wild blind white eyes
she hisses in your direction
opium smoke, glazed eyes
carnivorous hands
tongue long and licking
Eve moves beneath him like a viper

LILITH

you looked on to Eden first
angel of the morning
stretched owl claw and wing
until they tried to catch you
clipping your blood feathers
preventing flight, escape
pulled you down into the hungry maws
three bodies conjoined in rhythmic movement
in revolution, ravenous—insatiable
you became a body only
a bridge linking the two
an appendage
don't look into the faces
Eve commands you
to the floor with a finger
over many days
this is the only way
you can see her—
pale red
between limbs
salty mouth
smoke

she

jerks

out

the

bones

pulls on Adam's ribs

one   by   one

inserting

through

the thin membrane

of her core

into her chest

your skin grows

ashy over the days

and months

your feathers and teeth bleed, dry, fall

peeling large bloody scales

it is hard to move in the desert

men are still when they look in your direction

Eve blows plumes

her scent on the wind

she has them all

they know her body

eventually

no cure

disintegration

floating on juniper wind

terraforming
Sahara sand
you wander
lonely
detached
until you find Lilith bathing
birthing magnificent creatures in her cave
her feathers are luminescent, thick and strong
she shows you how to let the teeth grow in
prodding gums unashamed with finger
she explains that you were never
meant to lay upon your back.
you chose who to let in
not gods of secret sin
did he say no?
why should he?

fly and fly again

A Work in Progress

she painted
slants of light
you rested
without a word
posing
like a lover might do
like a bought supplicant
silent
pliant
serpents slither
through your eyes
you exhibit
the patience of a saint
it is perfection
a bliss of sorts
to paint you
propped up with wire
you used to cry
but you learned
silence is better
stasis is observed
in perfection

the restraints

gone now

blood brown

dry eclipsing your feet

like a discarded dress

i'll make you beautiful, she said

i'll make you shine

And she kept her word

glazing your skin in urethane

IMPULSE

you loved
like a serial killer
impulse

stalking barefoot
just behind

imprinted
focused mind

slice the skin
pull the bone

slip-on in
I am stone

you loved
like a serial killer
impulse

breathless dark
no space to borrow

close and warm
skintight sorrow

hear me sing
into oblivion

broken wing seraphim
anti-lover Abaddon

you loved
like a serial killer
impulse

Home

the house spreads her legs

opens her mouth

ghosts swing on breath

moving through cracked glass

slipping through bullet holes

rimmed in blood

rings of cut teeth

from the first iteration

passing through flesh

passing through glass

until cocooned in the wall

spirit wrapped in lead

festooned deep

into wood

spirit fusing

into the glue

arching up the slats

into the shingles

until mouth on mouth

they were one

they are one

COPPER

In *Prompt Magazine* 2021

copper pennies

wet on lip

cheek cold

warmth transfers

my head was made for this space.

the vein throbs~~~

i picture it blue before the oxygen.

before my teeth pricked it, slicing it in two.

the picture changes

my mouth settles

tiny tubes, one red, the other blue.

the smell is metallic

amber musk.

i pull in your odor

i draw in the warmth

your blood in tandem

is this how alcohol used to feel

i don't know you

i took you

i am hungry.

B-GIRLS

every time i   take

i think of your name

this is how   i startle them

i call

your

name,

your name

they stop

aware—not alone

i slide

behind them

sniff the neck

butterflies of tension

but never resist

hushed orange leaves twirling

lips, line of skin, and hair

rough bumps

under my lips

i say your name

your name   your name

driving it into flesh—licking salt

pulling hard

blood

teeth

tributaries

she sighs

arching like a ladle

twisting like a handle

she doesn't know

she is dying.

i weep tears between   pressed against her

lay below her body

until cold

until the sun rises

revolutions into the west

CROW MAN

crow man
streetlamp
book in hand
half-remembered cigarette
formaldehyde burn
pulled from crevice
of brick and lip
yellow light
falling down
yellow light
husky sound
of greasy feather
dirty hair
morphing
into red
like he sits on a wire
ignored by those
below

asylum club
never moving
even when a girl got stabbed

fell right before him

her last breath

finger reaching

hand open

painful clicks

palmed

on his shoe

he didn't look up

just reached out

touched the fingers one by one

she swore the brick bare

wet brick

no one there

I KNOW

the wicket snapped
in dark of night
my fingers reach
orb dim light
i know she comes for me
flat and still
holding breath
scent of rose
scent of death
i know she comes for me
creaking plank
flowing hair
glowing fire
in the air
i know she comes for me
crawling up
between my feet
her immortal hands
slink and cling
i know she comes for me

Stone

fire on the mountain
full moon of the first
your daughters will hunger
your daughters will thirst
missing girl posters
snap in the wind
sun brittle paper
tender for fire
of drum circle men
watch the gnarled hand
keepers of time
play, but don't tell
dance till you die
mothers mourning
quietly done
village of happiness
darkness hidden by sun
red tents do not hold them
nor the Spanish Creek
they vanished, you see
the girls that you seek
our priestesses are dancing

among all your lords
intentions wide enough
so they can sink in
lowering bodies
violet mouth &fingers
into the mines
into her teeth
the mountain licks
her tiny sharp teeth

A DREAM

i had a dream she said
of the Sangre de Cristo
they were crimson, so red

her mouth
terrible teeth
siphoning hole

from it, they arose
red women with obsidian knife

followed by the men
who shapeshifted
into creatures of the night
hunting their daughters
hunting their wives
haunting the edge of pinyon

red women dancing around yucca

their hunger had no end
their hunger had no end

i had a dream she said

please help it to end
the mountain she cries out
she is hunger without end

you

you were never a martyr

you were an open coat

cold influx of air

silk on the throat

A hand in my hair

Everyone has left

You~~~ and you and you

flitter

ghost

reflection

a cold lie

projecting

like a spell

of teal paint to keep

the monsters at bay

but you are just a house

the wind sings through

broken window

enduring pain

You~~~ and you and you

COIL

world on fire
the words
they curl
around
glowing arcs
spitting gold
dripping red
coming
in my mouth
i swallowed them down
i wanted to be fed

coiled there
slither on belly
twist the fate
give up darling
write the hate

hot blood traded
gambled free
open body
bloody knee

hacked up pieces
hacked up bride
half a women
you might try to hide

eyes are locking
can't skip truth
tower of records
close to you
biology babble
words like love
words like trouble
to make her come

introductions
whisky creeper
cigarettes
alchemy
ether
i called you dragon
last i saw
shovel of dirt
open lips
you shoved your words
deep
with dirty hands

CHILD

child of the night, flick of the lighter
calling to the darkness that claws up inside her
you are the one who never knew

child antenna, thorax and wing
fangs, venom, barbs that would sting
you are the one who never knew

child of claw, slice of the lung
the meat of the marrow frightfully won
you are the one who never knew

child of the faun, horn of the cruel
cracking the bones blood glittering jewel
you are the one who never knew

child of broken deformed bone
child of madness demented home
you are the one who never knew

child who dances under the moon
sadness spoke in broken tune

you are the one who never knew
the thing coils in my belly
the breath bubbles there

its shoulders pop
settling between the ribs

HAUNTED

slippery silence
outside obtuse
fractured glass
within walls
invisible data
inside the container
porous terra cotta
i picture language
tongues of green flame
like the movies
like numb children
they glitch sometimes
in the wavering loops
digital monochrome
i do the same
my voice gathers data
my voice trembles on the phone
reduction
arithmetic to English
with eyes glued closed
my mouth sewn
in fiber

in stitches

breath burning

gaping mouth

penetration

of cool damnation

Eris, Monster, Mother, Queen

static of the in-between

slipstreams of silence

tinnitus tremor

haunted home

tapping the wall

in a modern morse code

bile in my mouth

footfall through the apocalypse

we tread so carefully

don't we

to keep the sleeping monsters quiet

EPAR

for this is a court of law

he eyes you across the way

sneering in the actual now

as he ever did in memory

frozen then

frozen now

like you organically became a part of the wood

they disrobe you once more

on dais above

why didn't you speak up?

they ask

they always ask

there are reasons you think

but you don't say

the crime being

the only one

victims must prove

beyond reasonable doubt

things that happen

behind closed doors

questions that race from memory

racing down the hall

as you wanted

but could not

articulate

down your throat

into your body

you recoil

push back trauma

erase hands

fingerprints

that are not yours

that time

you were a small child

screaming

he the monster

he walked away

you faded faster

into the gloom

tightly wound

beneath the ground

swallow the dirt

sin of the body

sin of the Earth

captured bird

damaged womb

Full Moon

he got purgatory
he got probation
she got the forever things
nightmare mastication
the ink that won't move
deep in the flesh
sins on the mountain
sins in the ash
buried under the fire
no one will ever hear you scream
as you push up
on the bottom of boots
stomping in americana rhythm
pressing into the grave
they can't hear you screaming
they don't hear you rave
you are the voiceless terrified girl
they hushed you up
They Kill, Kill Kill
the men with their drums
around the full moon circle
snakes in your mouth

viper at ankle

they thought the stones would bring silence

until they heard you sing

like water in creek stone

rolling pain

someone will see

there in the dark

they buried you shallow

under aspen bark

fingers weave curses

lips alchemy

You say very quietly, "hear me."

BABYLON

skin,

the thin sheeting

that hides so much rot

she was atrophied before

i peeled that flesh, peeled the fat

she was beautiful in a way that birds are

delicate, huge eyes, feathers tattooed down her hip

peacock feathers, i think

male birds she emulated

drunk on power

pretty sure

it never occurred to her

the ancient DNA

birds and beaks

razor-sharp teeth

when i killed her

i pulled the knife through

it didn't make sound

no ripping like canvas

no feeling like a zipper

some resistance as i went deeper

deeper than i ever did before
she had so many layers
i thought i knew it all
but there was so much to explore

La Leth Laughs

if i haunted the wood, there
on the mountain's bloodied teeth
where she yawns wide
pickaxe rusted into stalactite uvula
it is beyond in dark I lay
between her yellowed bones
he left me half of a whole
there in the dark so long ago
La Lethe laughs—i hear her
stonehard, shiver
my weeping stopped long ago
her veins of silver and quartz
drop deep in this mine
crawling winged beasts
they swing above
supersonic speeches in echoes
little bites—small ones
my blood ingested
feeding the mums and the pups
the leathery wings shaken out
bloated belly of spirits
my skull rolled deeper into her mouth
La Lethe laughs—i hear her

ẎTSIRHC

smell the damp

earth and bones

people walked over me

no one knows I weep

my fingers traced

the soil

six feet above

they seemed not to smell

the veil of the dead

I floated around them

they can't feel my wet tongue

sometimes

I hear their voices in my head

whispers

desperate annotations

obliterations

prayers

agitations

the swish of blood

miles of tributaries

webs across their bodies

maddening in a way

a thirst for salt

a thirst for water

I hunger for something half-remembered

they say death is profound

but it is boredom in dark

lost wandering,

feeding hopelessness

desire is my companion

more than you ever were

sunlight and sorrow

every tomorrow

in the time that knew you

my cadaverous soul did not bend

to the curve of your rib

though you ate me—yes you did

I exist in a twilight that is the layers of the Earth

time half-remembered tangled

in jagged edges

my madness where light and love shimmered

my fingertips raw blood

under asphalt

where I trace your name

—Ÿtsirhc

Argona

i did not close the door

heaven in the feather
all it required was a dagger
tipped over the heart
even if carved, thin fingers apart

he stood by and watched
maker, shaker, creator
energy siphoning out of soul
return to the fount, drown in the hole

to see rotten things buried under bone
oh, the horror of the final truth

he was a father, lover to you
eyes cut from head, oh what a shame
laughing at her pain
laughing over grave

and you were too foolish to see
now just a ghost in a closet of stars

discarded bones, parts in mason jars

broken they left you
aroused with the fire
cautiously waiting for ashes to float higher
knocking on the door of your ribs, pull them wide

i did not die

doused in the water
infused with hot pain
dripping in the baptism of a second coming

never one to behave
or silently go
too terrible to silence, too heavy to throw

do you ask for absolution?
in moments of silent night
end of an era, ending of light

BONES OF WORD, BONE OF FEATHER

sometime in the night, the engineer froze

his hands rolled off the tools

broke the bone

interests favored

the cooling of mechanisms

quiet of cogs

paper and pen

wings and bones of birds

tattooed words on feathers

until he could render

plans in tiny squares

of mathematical sheets of paper

etched into the white yellow

of honeycombed marrow

climbing over massive radioactive magnets

multi minutes for introspection

madness, words spilled

time to time on the tiny boxes

nine by eight joined until bigger

scratches, scrawls, doodled goodbyes

poetic fashion

plagiarized characters

smoking cigarettes

hot whisky numbed tongues

fractured narrative

compressed in the collider of his mind

atoms smashing in infinitive

looking for his own version of the god particle

a flaw in the machine

to expose

explode the eyes and blow the brain

obliteration of logic a cost of fully dreaming

monochrome has purpose, ultimate introspection

why is memory always gray?

a reincarnation without ever having to bleed or die

or rise—

outlined imagined stories of goodbye

speak the words

incantation

stir the fingers there and there

trace around hip and breast

in comparison to the writer

neither God nor a martyr

NINAVA

Ninava slips between the voices
between the floorboards
song interrupted,
fingers slender
reaching for his soul

she touches his heel
wants him to stumble
his love, selfish, brutal
tied wrists, gagged mouth
he laid her there to remember tomorrow
but that was many years ago
pale darling, lovely body
rotting on the bone
older now, he remembers
others left him all alone
Ninava waits beneath the floorboards
dust floats on lightened beam
she waits for him to love her
waits for him to explain
why he put her below
years ago, after sweet mountain rain

POISON WOMAN

on the mesa

crumbled adobe

perverse on sand

blood struck

burnt offering

spiders eat the eggs

whispered incantations

cuts along the legs

kiss her poison lips

her tongue tastes of Earth

her skin sienna charcoal

coyote father birthed her

from a seed and dung

laughter in

sunrise transformation

only to live as day is long

she knew her part

cut sacred arc

gapping wrists

open in bloody yawn

veins a dark connection

serpents in the sand

out on the mesa
rocks began to churn
rolling down into the Rio Grande
sunset salutation
as water began to burn

Opio~Cordyceps

the spawn threw out tiny white threadlike roots

within the chest cavity of man

easily supported in incubation.

thriving in the warm dark places in his cheek

conquest of the corners of his eyes

the spores fed and bubbled over

populating mycelium growing

out of the decomposition of his body

he could not recall the exact moment of infection

though he tried to remember

he could not locate the time when the parasite first spoke in his mind

it seemed as if it had always resided there

whispering with harsh syllables.

he would stand at the mirror, arms at his sides

trying to see blurred, in broken fractal

the metamorphosis was in small bites at first

eating the live cells of his body in unmissed portions

long threads stretching out

replication process in parallel

following the thick tube of his aorta

dark browns and black spores entangling

looping around vein and organ

sometimes when he breathed
the oxygen flowed over the papery ribs of gills
preparing something just behind his tongue
fungi spoke words in poetics
songs of consumption

his wife, at first, thought this was an anxiety
or an allergy to something buried in the fertile soil
she plunged her hands into the dark, searching
soft textures rebounded like sponge
adhering to her own skin
she thought this was love
he endured her fingers
the prodding, swirling
he loved her as a mother but hated her as a wife
she moved through rooms with a heaviness
wrapping vine-like arms around him twice, sweaty and hot
lichen developing silently
chewing away at her epidermis
he watched it with wonderment
in the night, she opened like a flower
under his slow love
thin membrane swallowing
pseudo placenta, warmth, blindness
she did not fear him then
entreating him into the sun
as he pulled her below the soil

he thought the spores at first were flaking skin
but they were earthy in color
browns and greens and hard black crusts
he transferred into the air around them
his hunger for broken things increased
the symbiotic voices were growing louder
giving in to the need to expand
parasitic ticking voices feelings of madness
shedding and expanding
atrophied tissue orgasmic bliss
when he made love to her
it never felt like his body at all
spawning in the dark
molting the spores
and when they got heavy
they would peel off floating
sickly greens, browns, fuzzy, soft, spreading.

she began her transformation
into a thicker weed with wild white flower
thorns pushed out of the skin
thick with repellent oil
until she could cut
until he simply slid off
the sharp edges serrated the fuzzy group of eukaryotic organisms
she stretched out of the sac
walked upright on weak legs like a calf

in those last moments of union

she chewed her way out

back into the sun

she sprouted white flowers of snakeroot

he instead opened more of himself

fungal population of his body

the fungi spread within the tributaries of blood

crossed the brain barrier

mind-controlling symbiosis

the spores did not stop

they built up behind the papery ribs of gills,

forcing his mouth open and on his hot breath traveled

every time the man thought he had finished molting

the process would start again

shrug off his flesh spreading

scratching symbiotic whispers followed,

folded into his brain

transmutation, far too dangerous to hunt, touch, or eat.

DECEMBER MOTHER

she weeps within the water

vocals across the berm

of broken boulders

slanted aspen

cottonwoods twisted old over ice

she calls for her children

in clicks and gurgles

smashing open palms

on molecules of cold glass

i hear her

she is not mine

i hear her

the lilt of song

the sorrow song

bubbles trapped

to small breath

fingers tracing words

of retribution

there is peace among curses

power in hate

lips part blue

floating black spider webs

distorted under cold glass

screaming but only i receive it

echoes burrowing into ear

winter worm

drawn to the edge

will it crack beneath boot?

shall i wade in

wrap my arms around whitened corpse

let her pull me in

i trail above the ice

she is pulled like a moving screen

dragging further south

her body blue and pale

water in silent movement

below the hoar frost sky

i hear her

hands over ears

her children are not here

nothing of note but falling snow

no animals in the wood

nothing to save her

as nothing ever could

doomed to flow

below this ice

a form of retribution

a mother who drowned her child

for food in dead of winter

i hear her
but cannot save her
the child in her stomach
far beyond the womb
the child suffers silently
in the mother
of December moon

TIAMAT DREAMING

abandoned she lies

pivoted by her sex

overtaken

languid

exhausted

saddened

a remembrance

a lost violent moment

of creation

climax and death

dreams behind the wall of her skull explode

throws open the door

a mysterious unvisited room

the door yawns wide like hips connected to thighs

brain waves flow out of the opening

a slow rotation

sleep paralyzed in a cushioned cocoon

lovely tries to move her limbs

she pushes the gel-like membrane

digging nails into the soft peach-like flesh

inhaling, her mouth fills with jelly

no air

limbs twist

panic

nails rake upon the barrier

ribbons of membrane peeling

she covets air

no release from the compressing pod

every breath siphons more gel into mouth and lungs

sweet and choking

digging toes and fingers deeper into the soft flesh

until her toes slide through a small slit

frigid air swallows foot and calf

gravity-fastened teeth into the thigh

pulling down into the bottom of the pod

out of the torn opening

she falls, gasping for breath.

choices dissect as she spools into the great orchestra of unconsciousness

carried along with erratic firing of her brain

tentacles—greedy

cup her body in suction, a greater force of gravity pulling her down

heartbeats within the chest— hushed

thinning into strange vibrational bubbles that only exist below the sea

an infinite expanse of subconscious dims her eyes

floods her senses

a suicide (is it too late?) but you changed your mind

circular ridges compress around the body

relax as if within the gullet of a snake

darkness closes inward, squeezing into a single atom

electrons cycling, trying to expand beyond the valence shell

a hopeless attempt to participate in covalent bonding.

Tiamat struggles alone with this pain

sucks in a breath, but breath doesn't feel real in this space

hovering in nothingness so black only her awareness umbilicated to

something unnamed

what remains—uncertain.

touching fish-like bodies wiggling, nibbling her skin

sensations keep changing, warping what she knows to be her body

amniotic air percolates, bubbles of warmth rush to her lungs

pulling her knees and arms inward, she explodes outward

hands and feet sliding against another membrane

three more times, and something breaks

spilling her out, somersaulting across a cold hard surface

where had she been?

afterbirth gushing around pooling into a new shadowed space

face down, gasps for air

eyes flick open, rolling over onto her back

above, the ceiling resembles the top plate of a mouth, rigid and

yawning

her tongue runs across the top of her own

tries to speak

her voice rough and echoing throughout the strange chamber

she pushes, arms tremoring, barely able to support her weight

long heavy skirts cover her legs, the torn edges damp

her breasts drop uncovered in the way of ancient Minoan bull dancers

braids hanging limply to her waist as she reaches out trembling hands under the dim light

glimmering pools of blood-stained amniotic water on the floor

frustrates her attempts

to stand

weak legs stabilize beneath the weight of soaked velvet skirts

tentatively she steps—her foot catching at the hem

she stumbles, her hands flattening on a wall of wet stone, fuzzy with

lichen

the fungi spread following seams of rough-hewed squares

rusted sound twisted out of the dark, at first a scraping

like a blade on ice, then it dipped low, growling

she could feel a menacing presence beginning to take shape beyond the

ability of her eyes

to see

Lovely trusts the safety of the dream and hitches up the dress in her

fists

curious instinct pulls towards the sound

animal instinct—the same trait that kills cats and moths

and sends the elk racing over cliff's edge

Her steps close the gap between her earthy body and the wall of

undecipherable vantablack eschewing senses, enacting a scintillating

sensation

danger felt laughable in a dream

long bony fingers reach from the dark

fingers clutched at the air, curling then extending

the unnamable thing reaches for a waiting hand

claws reaching out from the dark

her spine tingles, hair of her body erect
the ground wobbles, her thighs are warm
"not real," she whispers
terribly real, she thought
the god made the world out of her

Awake Now

my fellow carnivore

my comrade

blood brother

i hunger for the hunt with you

running in the night

breath and blood pumping

teeth tearing

hunger never-ending

until we must awake

we cannot always dwell in the nighttime

You never die in a dream. Do you?

About the Author

Brenda S. Tolian, DA, MFA, is a New Orleans-based author whose work pulses with her surroundings' vibrant and eerie energy, whether she writes of the southwestern desert or the French Quarter. As the author of Blood Mountain, published by Raw Dog Screaming Press, Brenda has carved a unique niche in the literary world, blending haunting narratives and poetry with inspiration from the gothic, folk horror, and the grotesque. She writes the Queer, dark, and philosophical exploring the places rarely talked about with visceral symbolism. Her work has been featured in numerous anthologies and publications, representing her talent in contemporary, academic, and dark literature.

Tolian holds degrees from Adams State University, a Creative Writing MFA from Regis University, and a Doctorate in English Literature Pedagogy from Murray State University.